To Mom, who inspired my creative side, and Dad, who
taught me to think for myself, to keep moving forward,
and to not bang my head against the big rock
—R.D.

To John and Andrew. Thanks for helping me fly like a butterfly
—T.B.

Acknowledgments:
Hugs to my creative kids, Alexis and Matt, who make me think differently;
Kisses to my love and friend, Nancy who drives me, inspires me, and is always there
with me; Josie Yee; Kelsey Skea; Tracy Bishop; Tom Francisconi; and SirSpeedy.
Special thanks to Susan Lurie who made Pipsie better every time she touched the story.
—R.D.

A LURIE INK Book

Published by Two Lions, New York
www.apub.com

Amazon, the Amazon logo, and Two Lions are trademarks of Amazon.com, Inc., or its affiliates.

ISBN-13: 9781477826300

ISBN-10: 1477826300

Library of Congress Control Number: 2014918307

Design by Tanya Ross-Hughes

Printed in Mexico

First Edition

10 9 8 7 6 5 4 3 2 1

PIPSIE
nature detective

THE DISAPPEARING CATERPILLAR

Written by Rick DeDonato
Illustrated by Tracy Bishop

two lions

It was a beautiful morning at Pipsie's house.

Pipsie wiped the sleepies from her eyes
and looked at Alfred Z. Turtle.

She saw something SO SILLY, she had to
rub the sleepies from her eyes again.

Alfred had a row of STRIPES right down
the middle of his head.

Pipsie looked at him closely. "Alfred, I think
you're turning into a TIGER."

Alfred walked over to his mirror
s—l—o—w—l—y
(that's how turtles walk)
and looked up.

As sure as the shell
on his back, there were
YELLOW and BLACK
stripes on his head!

Pipsie took out her magnifying glass.
After all, she was a nature detective.

"It's a baby caterpillar," she said.
"She's smiling at me . . . and she has BIG BLUE EYES
and the cutest DIMPLES!"

"Hi! My name is Frannie," the caterpillar said.
"Can I be your friend?"

"That would be EXCELLENT," Pipsie replied.
"I love making NEW FRIENDS. And Alfred does, too!"

Pipsie, Alfred, and Frannie
became excellent friends.
For the next week,
they played silly games,
like I'M FRANNIE!

But most of the time, Frannie just ate and ate and ate
and grew bigger and bigger and BIGGER.

In ten days, Frannie was more than 1,000 times BIGGER
than the day she met Pipsie and Alfred.

"If I grew as much as Frannie," said Pipsie, "I would be GIGANTIC!"

One morning, Pipsie woke up extra early,
ready to play, but Frannie had VANISHED!
Where could she be? Pipsie wondered.

"Alfred, we have a mystery to solve!" Pipsie said.
"Without a doubt, we'll figure this out! Let's go!"

Pipsie and Alfred looked in DARK and ICKY places. . . .

She's not in here. PU-WEE.

WOWEE! I love peanut butter and jelly!

. . . and SWEET and STICKY places.

Alfred looked inside Pipsie's hat.

Pipsie looked inside Alfred's shell.

"No Frannie anywhere."

Pipsie but
no Frannie.

Pipsie climbed up to her Detective Tree House
to get her nature-detective tools.

"Put on your detective cap, Alfred. It's time
to hunt for clues. Frannie liked the garden.
Let's start there."

"Look, Alfred. These leaves are all chewed up.
I bet Frannie ate them."

"I have a nose for clues—and this smells like a clue!
We need to find out more about these leaves.
FOLLOW ME!"

I have a nose
for lunch—and those
leaves smell delicious.

Pipsie and Alfred went to the insect garden at
the zoo to learn more about the leaves.
They saw a plant exactly like the one in Pipsie's yard.
It was called milkweed.

"Wow! Caterpillars sure love milkweed," Pipsie said.
"Hey, Alfred, you can't eat that! That's our clue!"

"I wonder what that green dangly thingy is," Pipsie said.

"That's a CHRYSALIS," said a man with a colorful badge.

Alfred read the badge. It said, "Ask Me About Bugs."

"We're looking for our friend Frannie the caterpillar,"
Pipsie said. "Can you help us? We met her two
weeks ago—and last night she vanished. Poof! Gone!"

"Look for a chrysalis like this," the man said.
"Keep watching it—and you'll find Frannie.
But she'll look very different!"

"Come on, Alfred! Let's make this mystery history!"

Pipsie and Alfred rushed home s—l—o—w—l—y
(because that's how turtles rush).
And they found a chrysalis hanging in their backyard!

They checked it every day for nine days.
On the tenth day, Pipsie looked at it real closely. . . .

. . . and a monarch butterfly came FLYING out!

Pipsie looked at the butterfly's BIG BLUE EYES.
Then she noticed the cute DIMPLES.
"Look, Alfred. It's our Frannie! We found her!"

Look!
I can fly!

FUN FACTS

1. In only 2 WEEKS, a baby monarch caterpillar grows several thousand times its size. Then it goes into a chrysalis and becomes a butterfly.

2. The female butterfly is larger than the male butterfly.

3. Most caterpillars eat a variety of plant leaves. Monarch caterpillars eat only milkweed leaves to grow. When they become monarch butterflies, they eat the nectar from many other flowering plants, including milkweed. Milkweed can be poisonous to other insects and birds, but not to monarchs. In fact, it protects them. After the monarchs eat the milkweed, it makes them taste really bad. Some birds might throw up if they tried to eat a monarch!

4. Caterpillars LOVE to eat. They'll even eat the shell they hatch from!

5. Caterpillars eat so much and grow so fast that their skin gets too tight. They shed their skin five times so they can keep growing.

6. Did you know that butterflies taste with their feet? When they land on a flower, they can tell if it will be good for them to eat!

Continue the fun with Pipsie at www.pipsienaturedetective.com.

Insect insight by Jess King, entomologist